CONTENTS

I'd forgotten how much I hate this kingdom. The fields full of crops. The clear blue skies. The simple, smiling people, going about their petty lives.

Well, all that is about to change. When I get my hands on the Book of Derthsin, *I will have a whole new world of evil magic at my fingertips.*

King Hugo will pay for his smugness. Avantia will tremble. Its protector Beasts will suffer. But above all, it is Tom who will feel my wrath.

And as he perishes, it will be my smiling face he sees.

It's good to be back!

Malvel

THE UNNATURAL STORM

Tom leaned low over Storm's back,
his eyes narrowed against the
howling wind and driving rain.
Elenna, in the saddle behind Tom,
clung tightly to his waist. Storm's
huge, feathered wings beat hard,
carrying them swiftly through the
night. Tom felt a rush of gratitude

towards Lyra, the young witch from Henkrall who had given Storm the magical wings. Without her help, the journey would have been almost impossible.

Dark, tattered clouds streamed past as they flew, and above the roar of the wind in his ears, Tom could hear the crash and boom of waves far below. The first blood-red glimmer of dawn streaked the eastern sky, and looking down, Tom could just make out the slender line of shadow they were following, cast on to the raging ocean. He and Elenna had already defeated two Beasts, summoned by Malvel from the Netherworld using the stolen

Book of Derthsin. After each victory, a magical totem had sprung up from the ground, casting a long shadow directing them towards the next stage of their Quest. This time, the totem's shadow led south. And if the last two Beasts were anything to go by, Tom knew Malvel would have summoned something truly evil to face them.

Gusts of wind tore at Tom's hair and clothes as Storm swooped over heaving waves that pounded in a wild fury against the shoreline.

"Someone's in trouble!" Elenna cried, pointing. Through the towering cascades of spray thrown up by the huge breakers, Tom could

see a jumble of huts on the shore.
Scurrying figures dragged fishing
boats up the beach, away from

the crashing waves. The smashed remains of several boats already churned in the shallows.

"Without Sepron to calm the waters, the villagers are at the mercy of the storm," Elenna shouted over the wind.

Tom glanced at his shield. All the magical tokens there, including Sepron the Sea Serpent's green scale, had faded to a dull grey. Malvel had cast a spell, sending the wizard Aduro and all the Good Beasts into a death-like sleep. Until Daltec and Lyra found an antidote to the spell, Tom could no longer call on the Beasts for aid.

Tom's chest tightened at the

thought of delaying their Quest, but he had no choice. "We have to help them," he said. As Storm swooped lower, Tom kept his eyes on a knot of struggling villagers. A flash of lightning bleached his vision. Thunder boomed right overhead, making Tom tense up, half expecting to be hit.

"Rafe!" An anguished cry pierced though the thunder's echoing rumble. "Rafe!"

A tall woman stood among the breaking waves, her long hair and sodden clothes whipping about her as two broad men tried to pull her towards the shore. The pain in the woman's eyes as she gazed out to the churning ocean made Tom's pulse quicken. *Someone's lost at sea!*

Storm landed on the beach at a canter, kicking up wet sand, then pulled to a stop. Tom and Elenna swung from the saddle and waded into the crashing waves. Icy water sucked at Tom's legs, tugging and slapping all round him. The struggling woman sobbed breathlessly, fighting against the two men that held her.

"But Rafe! He'll drown," she cried.

"No use you going down alongside him, Sally," one man answered gruffly, his weather-beaten face creased with pity.

"Hey!" the second man shouted,

frowning at Tom and Elenna, "What are you kids doing out here? You'll drown!"

"We can help you," Tom said. "I'm Tom, Master of the Beasts, and that is my horse." Tom pointed to where Storm stood on the beach, his huge wings folded across his back.

The man's eyes widened as they rested on the stallion. His jaw went slack. "Well, I'll be…" he muttered.

"Please!" The woman, Sally, grabbed Tom's tunic. "My husband, Rafe. His fishing boat never came in…"

Tom nodded. "Get to safety," he shouted. "We'll do what we can." He whistled high and loud. Storm

plunged through the breaking waves
towards them. Tom and Elenna leapt
up on to his back. With a powerful

flap of his magical wings, the stallion climbed skywards.

In the growing light of dawn, Tom scanned the chaos below looking for any sign of the missing skiff. Each massive swell surged up towards them, then sucked away, only to rise again higher than before. *Could anyone really be alive out here?*

Suddenly Elenna let out a cry. "There!" She lifted a hand and pointed further out to sea. Tom gasped. *Are we too late?* The water ahead swirled and funnelled sharply into a wide, steep-sided whirlpool. Tom could see broken planks of wood spinning in the current, and a sodden figure lay draped over a splintered

spar, drifting towards the vortex.

"Rafe!" Elenna cried. "The whirlpool's going to drag him down!"

SEA RESCUE

Tom urged Storm lower towards
the stranded man, steering him
between the waves. A fierce gust of
wind caught Storm's wings, making
them buckle. Tom's stomach lurched
as Storm plummeted towards the
ocean, but the brave stallion lifted
his head and whinnied, pumping his
wings, steadying their flight.

"Rafe!" Tom shouted to the limp figure. The man didn't stir. Tom shouted once more. "RAFE!" But it was no use. He could hardly hear his own voice against the raging of the wind and sea. "We have to go lower!" Tom cried.

Storm's mighty wings beat with powerful thrusts, bringing them closer to the churning water.

"Rafe!" Tom yelled, shouting so fiercely his throat felt raw. This time the wind must have carried his cry, for the man below slowly lifted his head. His eyes focussed for a moment on Tom, then fluttered closed again. Rafe's head sank back on to the wooden spar.

He's exhausted, Tom thought.

At that moment, two huge waves slapped together below, sending up a towering plume of water. Tom tugged on Storm's reins and the stallion swooped out of reach of the spray. "This is hopeless," Tom growled through gritted teeth. "We'll all be drowned if we get too close!"

"I have an idea," Elenna said, scrabbling suddenly in Storm's saddlebag. She pulled out a length of thick rope.

"Good thinking!" Tom said. He took the rope and shook it out. One end snaked down towards the stranded man.

"Grab on!" Tom shouted, keeping

the rope as steady as he could with one hand, while holding Storm's reins with the other. Rafe lifted his head towards the rope, eyes widening. He pushed off from the beam, reaching out for it. But a huge wave crested under him, dragging him away, and swallowing the wooden plank. Rafe's pale face turned up towards Tom, wild with terror, then he was dragged beneath the water.

No! Tom hitched the rope to Storm's saddle pommel, then pulled up the loose end and held it.

"What are you going to do?" Elenna asked.

"I'm going in," Tom said, and dived.

As Tom plunged down into the
icy water, the cold seemed to clamp
around him like a vice, crushing
his chest. He pumped his arms and

legs, forcing himself deeper. Already his chilled muscles felt sluggish and numb. The current pulled him in every direction. Dark water swirled before his eyes. Bubbles and silt clouded his vision so he could hardly tell which way was up, and he lost his grip on the rope. He pressed on, his ears popping with the pressure. *Where is he?* Something dark shifted below him. Tom reached out a hand and felt cloth. *Yes!* He yanked at the waterlogged material, hugging it to him, circling Rafe's broad chest with his arm. Then he kicked his legs with all his failing strength and forced himself towards the surface.

Tom broke through the waves and

gratefully sucked in a breath of air. Paddling with one arm, he shifted Rafe in his grip, making sure the man's face was above water.

"Tom! Here!" Elenna cried from above, dangling the rope. Tom made a grab for it. His hand felt rubbery with cold and he could barely feel the cord, but he kept his fist clamped tight about it as Storm tugged him and Rafe through the water. Waves slapped at his face, filling his nose and mouth, making him choke until his throat burned. He clamped his teeth together and held on, as Storm dragged him through the peaks of the chopping waves.

Finally, Tom felt sand beneath

him and stumbled up to his feet, dragging Rafe up too. Without the deep water to help keep him afloat, the man became a sodden weight. Tom spotted figures splashing towards him through the shallows – Sally and the two men who had pulled her to safety. Tom sagged with relief as they took Rafe from his arms. He stumbled after them towards the beach. Ahead, he could see Elenna and Storm coming in to land.

When Tom reached the shore, Elenna and Sally were already huddled over Rafe, shaking him and calling his name. A group of villagers watched on, silent and wide-eyed, cloaks drawn close against the driving rain.

Elenna gently moved Sally aside, then put her ear to Rafe's chest. "He isn't breathing," she muttered. Sally let out a wail, as Elenna bent and put her mouth to Rafe's. Tom saw the man's chest rise as Elenna forced air into his lungs. *Please let him be all right!* Sally wept and wrung her hands as Elenna gave Rafe another breath, then another. Suddenly the man let out a gurgle and started to struggle. Elenna propped him up, and he vomited out a great torrent of water, then sat gasping for breath.

Joyful cries went up from the

huddled villagers. They swept forwards, embracing Sally and supporting Rafe as he struggled to his feet. A tall, muscular woman with jet-black hair and keen grey eyes draped a blanket around Rafe's shoulders, then turned to Elenna. "You saved his life!" she said. The woman took Tom's hand, shaking it warmly. "I am Nora, head of the village. I can't thank you enough for what you have done. We've never come so close to losing one of our people to the sea. But then, we have never seen a storm like this. It came upon us last night without warning and has raged ever since. If not for you, we would be mourning Rafe

now. Were you sent by the wizard?"

Tom tensed. *Wizard? Could that be Malvel?* He and Elenna exchanged a look of alarm.

"What wizard?" Elenna said.

"He appeared just before you did," Nora answered. "He told us he could stop the storm if we helped him find the Good Beast Sepron. Well, a great sea serpent washed up at Sandy Cove yesterday – so I sent the wizard that way, though I fear the creature is dead."

Dread clutched hold of Tom's guts and squeezed. "Sepron's not dead," he told the woman. "He's trapped in an enchanted sleep. The wizard you met must be Malvel – an evil sorcerer, come to kill Sepron while he sleeps. If that happens, there will be nothing to prevent storms like this ravaging the coastline. I must stop him."

Nora paled. "He went that way," she said, pointing. "If you hurry, you will catch him."

Tom nodded. "Don't worry, we will."

A fierce mixture of anger and dread raged inside Tom, warming his blood as he and Elenna raced up the beach and vaulted into Storm's saddle. With a kick of Tom's heels, the winged stallion lifted them back up into the stormy sky.

They flew low through the wind and rain, following the shoreline of the Western Ocean. The magical totem's shadow-path ran directly below them. Before long, they crested a bank of dunes and found themselves gazing down at a sandy bay, lashed by rolling waves. Stranded on the beach, well above the tideline, lay a huge, green-scaled serpent.

Sepron!

Rather than coiled as if resting or asleep, the Beast's body lay slack, head lolling and eyes closed. A hooded figure hunched over Sepron's sleeping form.

Elenna gasped. "Malvel!" The wizard had something clutched in his hand that glowed with a sickly yellow light – something the shape of a blade.

"I have to stop him!" Tom pressed

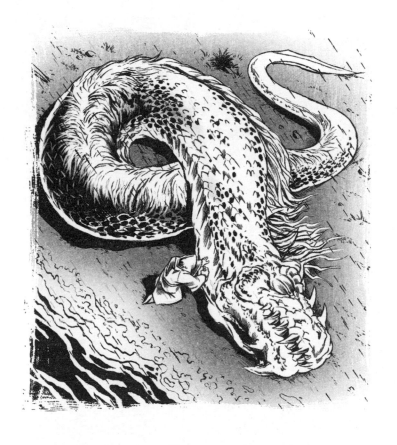

his knees into Storm's sides. He
could see the wizard on the beach
raising the glowing blade over
Sepron's giant head.

Tom unhooked his feet from Storm's stirrups. Just as the stallion swept low over the crouching wizard, Tom flung himself through the air...

1

CURING THE BEAST

Tom crashed feet first into the hooded shape, sending the wizard flying.

"Ow!" a voice cried. Tom hit the ground in a roll and leapt to his feet, reaching for his sword. He turned to see the wizard scramble up, brushing wet sand from his robe. As the man threw back his hood, Tom found himself staring into the rain-streaked face of his good friend, Daltec. The young wizard rubbed his elbow, wincing. "What was that for?" Daltec asked.

"Um…sorry," Tom said. "I thought you were Malvel."

"Well, in that case you're forgiven," Daltec said. "It's about time he got a good kicking!" Storm landed with a thud of hoofbeats nearby and Elenna leapt from the saddle.

"Daltec!" she said, running to join them. "What are you doing here?"

Daltec flourished the glowing yellow object in his hand, grinning. Tom could see now that it was a vial of liquid rather than a blade. "Lyra and I have made a potion we hope will wake the Beasts," Daltec said. "Lyra's gone to find Ferno. I was just about to administer the potion to Sepron…before I was so forcefully interrupted."

Tom winced apologetically. "How about Aduro?" he asked. The former wizard had been locked in a death-like sleep the last time Tom had seen him.

"The potion worked," Daltec said. "Aduro's still weak, but he should be fine, in time."

Tom felt as if a great weight had been lifted from his shoulders. He took a deep breath and smiled for what felt like the first time in a long while. "That is good news!" he said.

Elenna grinned too. "So, are you two just going to stand there chatting – or are you going to cure poor Sepron?"

Daltec nodded. "Of course – although I don't yet know if the potion will cure Beasts. We can only hope."

Tom, Elenna and Daltec stood beside the sea serpent's massive, long-toothed jaw. The Beast lay still, his scales slick with rain. Beneath a mottling of wet sand, Sepron's hide looked dull – almost grey. Tom reached out a hand and rested it on the serpent's brow. It felt as cold as stone. *I hope this works...*

Daltec lifted the vial in his hand
and slowly poured the glowing
liquid into one of Sepron's nostrils.

"The potion will take a few moments to start working," Daltec said. "While we wait, I should pass on some news from Tangala."

Elenna gasped. "King Hugo and Queen Aroha – and the baby!" she said. "Are they all well?"

"Oh yes," Daltec said. "As you know, the queen and king are now proud parents to a healthy baby boy. The king is on his way back to Avantia as we speak, to announce the good news to his people."

Tom frowned. "Surely with Malvel on the loose he'd be safer staying in Tangala."

"That's what I told him," Daltec said, "but you know what he's like.

He said his place is with his people."

Suddenly, Sepron let out a tremendous sneeze. Tom, Elenna and Daltec stepped back as the great Beast stirred and opened his ice-blue eyes. As Tom watched, a wash of colour spread across Sepron's hide from snout to tail. Like the shadow of a cloud passing from a meadow, his scales brightened to emerald green. The Beast lifted his massive head and gave it a furious shake.

All at once, Tom felt a strange ringing in his ears. It took him a moment to work out what it was. *Quiet!* The wind, which had howled and buffeted since they arrived, was gone. Gentle rain still pattered around them, but the air felt suddenly warm. Tom glanced out to sea. Sunlight pierced the clouds, turning the distant ocean from iron grey to burnished gold. Shielding his eyes from the light, Tom spotted a winged creature flying towards them. As it neared, he could make out the shape of a slender girl with large fluttering wings, like those of a butterfly.

"Lyra!" Daltec exclaimed. "She must have cured Ferno already."

Moments later, the young Henkrallian witch touched down lightly before them and folded her wings. She shook the rain from her short hair, then smiled. "Hello again,"

she said, extending a hand to Elenna, then to Tom.

"Avantia has much to thank you for," Tom said.

The girl looked down, her cheeks flushing red. "It's the least I could do," she said, knotting her fingers. "You've saved Henkrall from Beasts so many times."

"And now you've helped us save our Beasts," Tom said. "And Aduro. Not to mention that we have you to thank for Storm's wings."

At the mention of his name, Storm let out a snort and lifted his head.

"I'm glad he likes them," Lyra said. She glanced anxiously towards the sky as if eager to be away. "Now I must head north to find Arcta," she said, patting a satchel at her side, which clinked with the sound of glass vials knocking together. "I have Beasts to cure. Daltec – I'll leave Nanook to you."

"Thank you, Lyra," said Daltec, turning to Tom. "We should be back at the palace in time for the king's arrival two days from now. Good luck with your Quest, Master of the Beasts."

"And good luck to you," Tom said. Lyra gave Daltec a smile, then she nodded goodbye to Tom and Elenna, spread her colourful wings and fluttered away. When Tom turned back to Daltec, he saw the wizard surrounded by a shimmering haze of light – which disappeared, taking Daltec with it. With a flick of his long tail, Sepron also vanished, gliding into the calm blue ocean.

"Time for us to go too," Elenna said. She and Tom climbed on to Storm's back. Tom dug his heels into Storm's sides, and clung tight as the stallion leapt skywards. With the last wisps of cloud burning away and morning sun warming his face, Tom's spirits started start to lift – but then Elenna gasped and clutched his arm. "Tom!" she said. "If Hugo is two days south of Avantia, and heading north – doesn't that mean he'll cut right across the shadow path?"

Tom's heart gave a skip of fear. "You're right!" he said. "We have to find that Beast before it can harm the king!"

STRANGE WATER

Tom urged Storm onwards, his guts churning with dread at the thought of a Beast on the loose with the king nearby. *Why couldn't Hugo just stay put in Tangala? He's putting himself in grave danger.* The noonday sun beat down mercilessly as they flew, drying his clothes, but making Tom's skin prickle with sweat. The shadow path stretched away far beneath them, a thin line of darkness leading south. *If we really hurry, we might stop Malvel summoning the next Beast...* Suddenly, Tom realised with a pang of guilt that Storm's breath sounded harsh and laboured. The winged stallion had carried him and Elenna all morning, over fields and towns, farms and woodland. Now, a white foam of sweat streaked Storm's coat. *He's exhausted.*

"We'll have to stop," Tom told Elenna. Far below, a silver-blue ribbon looped through lush meadowland, glittering in the sun – the Winding River. Beyond that, the grassland quickly faltered, turning first to brown scrub, then harsh, red desert stretching all the way to the horizon. Soon there would be no more chance to take a drink.

"Time for a rest, boy," Tom told his horse. Storm's ears pricked and he let out a snort, then quickened his pace, swooping towards the glinting river. They landed neatly on the damp, mossy turf of the riverbank. A few hundred paces downriver stood a weathered stone bridge. On the far side of the river, beyond a thin line of parched trees and thorn bushes, the air above the desert dunes shimmered with heat. Tom and Elenna washed their dusty faces with cool water while Storm drank his fill then started cropping the grass near the water's edge.

"We'd better fill our bottles," Tom said, uncapping his canteen, then plunging it into the flowing water. Bubbles rippled up as water gurgled into the flask. Then, suddenly, Tom felt the bottle jerk in his hand as if tugged by a strong current. Tendrils of dark shadow swirled around it, like reaching fingers. Tom shuddered, snatching his flask from the water. The groping shadows remained, twisting in the shallows.

"Elenna, look," Tom said, pointing. Elenna frowned down at the sun-dappled surface.

"At what?" she asked.

"Those weird shadows," Tom said. "What's making them?"

Elenna shrugged. "It's just a trick of the light."

"Ow!" Tom jumped back, holding his stinging cheek. A silver fish flapped and flopped on the bank

at his feet. It had leapt right out of
the water, hitting him in the face.
Tom nudged the fish with his boot,
pushing it back into the water.

Elenna laughed. "That's what you
get for being paranoid," she said. Then
she too let out a yelp as a second fish
arced through the air, just missing
her. Then another hit the bank with
a slap, and another. Tom gasped and
stepped back as the whole bank
quickly became a mass of writhing
silver bodies.

"What is going on?" Elenna cried.

Tom shook his head in wonder,
backing away from the water's edge.
In the soft turf at his feet he spotted
an impression – a large boot print,

bigger than his own or Elenna's. Tom clenched his teeth.

"Someone's been here recently," he said, gesturing towards the print.

"Malvel," Elenna said. She glanced about warily. A high-pitched whinny from Storm made Tom spin, his pulse quickening. He found his stallion snorting and tossing his head, scuffing his hooves at the bank of the river as if readying to fight something Tom couldn't see.

Tom raced to Storm's side as the black horse reared and let out an angry neigh. "Easy now," Tom said, putting his hand on the stallion's flank and squinting into the water. He tensed. There was something down there. Something like a shadow but thicker – more solid, trailing just beneath the surface. It looked almost like tar.

Storm let out a terrified whinny. With a jolt of horror, Tom saw a thick strand of the strange, black gloop had wrapped tight about Storm's foreleg and was tugging him into the water. *The shadow's alive!*

"Elenna, help!" Tom called. He grabbed the stallion's reins. Storm scrabbled frantically at the bank. Tom fought to keep his horse from being dragged into the water. As Elenna raced towards him, he called on the strength of his magical breastplate. But despite all his

effort, the reins whipped through his hands, burning his palms. Storm plunged, eyes rolling and hooves flailing wildly, into the river.

1

5

TARANTIX

Tom leapt to the water's edge, his
heart thundering with shock as
Storm struggled and whinnied,
covered in inky sludge. The
stallion's kicking hooves sent up
globs of black filth as sticky strands
wrapped his body, binding his wings
to his sides.

"I'm coming, Storm!" Tom cried,

tugging his sword from its sheath. *I have to save him!* Tom bent his knees, ready to leap into the water.

"Tom! Wait!" Elenna called. He turned to see her pointing upstream across the river towards dense clump of bushes on the far bank. Shadowy tendrils oozed from between the thorny shrubs and flowed across the ground, pouring into the river.

"Well spotted!" Tom said. He called on the power of his golden boots and launched himself across the river, landing in a crouch beside the thicket. Vile black goo flowed past his feet, sending up a rancid stench. Tom drew back his sword and hacked at the stuff, but it flowed over and around his weapon, coating the blade.

"Tom! Look out!" Elenna cried, her voice shrill with fear. Tom glanced up to see that the bushes where the black goo led were shifting and rustling. He lifted his sword just as an enormous, bloated monstrosity barrelled into the open – a pale spider the size of a stagecoach. The Beast stood hunched on eight jointed white legs, six of which ended in a three-toed claw. Plates of pock-marked, greying bone covered its fat body and massive head, except for where a cluster of shiny eyes stared back at Tom with venomous

hate. The goo streaming across the ground flowed from a tapering point at the rear of the beast's abdomen. *It's some kind of spider silk!* Tom realised with disgust.

The monster reared up, its huge

curved fangs rasping together,
making a sound like a papery laugh.
Tarantix is hungry, the Beast hissed,
speaking through the red jewel
into Tom's mind, *and horse flesh is
sweet*. Tarantix's front legs whipped

out, yanking in the black web like a fishing net. Storm let out a panicked whinny, and Tom looked over to see the horse being dragged out of the river and on to the bank, encased in a thick cocoon of sticky strands.

Tom threw himself forwards, stabbing for the monster's vast, pale underbelly with his sword. *Crack!* A bony leg blocked his swipe with lighting speed. Tom barely registered a flicker of movement from the corner of his eye before another white limb smashed into his hip, throwing him sideways. He hit a tree stump and fell to the ground, winded.

"Tom! Take cover!" Elenna cried. Tom glanced up to see her standing on the bridge with an arrow aimed toward the Beast. He rolled behind the stump and crouched, gasping with pain. *Twang!* The first of

Elenna's arrows sliced through the rope of goo that bound Storm to the Beast, almost severing it. *Whoosh!* A second arrow followed the first. Then another. The remaining strands pinged away.

"Now chew on this!" Elenna cried, sending a final arrow whistling towards the Beast. It sank into the bony plate covering the creature's raised thorax. Tarantix hissed, her eight legs drawing quickly beneath her. She shot Elenna a look of pure hate. Then suddenly, her whirring limbs fell still. She lifted her head, her fang-tipped mouthparts trembling as if tasting the air.

I scent juicier prey than stringy

horse flesh. The Beast's voice snarled in Tom's mind. Tarantix turned and scuttled away in a blur of limbs towards the desert. Tom frowned after the Beast as she dwindled into the distance, throwing up clouds of red sand behind her. *Why would she just give up?* he wondered. Her words echoed in his mind. *Juicier prey...* Tom jolted to his feet, adrenaline fizzing through him.

"I think the Beast is going after King Hugo!" Tom called to Elenna. "I have to stop her."

"Go," Elenna said, crossing the bridge. "I'll free Storm." She fell to her knees beside the stallion and

started slicing away the black goo
with an arrow. "We'll catch you up."

Tom shot her a grateful look, then
spun on his heel and, calling on the
magical speed of his leg armour,
ran full tilt after the Beast.

6

ATTACK ON THE KING

Tom sped across the desert,
following the trail of churned-up
sand Tarantix had left in her wake.
Hot air shimmered all around him
and a relentless wind threw up
eddies of sand which scoured his
skin and stung his eyes. His legs
soon burned with the effort of

pounding over shifting dunes. But he ignored the pain, his thirst and the sweat dripping into his eyes. He focussed on the rhythmic thud of his boots, and of the blood in his ears. *I have to catch Tarantix before she reaches the king!*

Finally, Tom spotted a blurry red cloud of sand ahead of him in the distance. *Tarantix!* He forced himself to move faster and his aching lungs to suck in more air. Soon, Tom could make out the Beast's scuttling legs and broad, fat body. As he drew closer, the sand she kicked up filled his mouth with grit and made him squint. Tom let out a roar and leapt, hurling himself towards Tarantix's jointed hind leg. He threw his arms and legs around the bony limb and clung tight. The Beast let out a thin, furious screech, and kicked out. Tom's fingers slipped and he flew through the air. Powdery sand cushioned his fall. He leapt to his feet, ready to fight. But the Beast had rushed on, leaving a trail of red dust hovering above the desert. With a stab of dread, Tom spotted a second trail in the distance, heading at right angles to the Beast's. Calling on the enhanced vision of his golden helmet, Tom could clearly see a familiar green-and-gold coach surrounded by six armoured men. *No – the royal retinue!*

Adrenaline gave him new speed. With his eyes fixed on the Beast, the desert passed by in a blur. But ahead, Tom could see the Beast closing on the king's coach by the moment. *While there's blood in my veins, I won't let you harm him!* As soon as Tom came within striking distance of Tarantix's huge scuttling form, he drew his sword and swung it hard, hacking at a rear leg. *Crack!* The blade bit deep, and a jointed limb fell away, severed. Tarantix screamed like a lobster plunged into the cooking pot. Her remaining legs buckled and she tumbled over in the sand. She scrambled up and turned to face Tom on seven legs. *Ha! Not so fast now!* Tom's sword lashed out again. *Thwack!* Another leg lay twitching in the sand. Tarantix reared up to tower over him on her

remaining hind limbs, her fangs clacking together and her forelimbs spread wide.

You can't hurt me! Tarantix hissed. And as Tom watched, new legs telescoped out from stumps of the limbs he'd severed. His heart sank. *She can regenerate!* The Beast curled her abdomen beneath her, and a spurt of black goo shot towards Tom.

Tom dived and rolled clear, then leapt to his feet only to see more sticky strands jetting his way. He threw up his shield. It bucked in his hands as the goo struck, whipping round the edges, snagging it like a fly. The Beast dropped down on

all eight legs, then yanked on the
threads with her foreclaws, tugging
Tom's shield. Tom tightened his
grip and went with the movement,
letting himself be drawn towards
the Beast's pale mouthparts and
long curved fangs. *She must have a
weak spot...*

As Tom lurched over the sand, he
swung his sword weakly, as if vainly
trying to strike a blow. Then, when
the Beast's deadly fangs curved
above him, he sliced through the
gloop that trapped his shield, and
jabbed his sword upwards, between
the fangs into the Beast's soft,
glistening mouthparts. Tarantix let
out a deafening squeal. Her limbs

flailed, digging up sand, kicking it
into Tom's eyes. He blinked it away,
only to see the monstrous Beast
burrowing frantically downwards,
red sand already closing over her

pale, fat body. He leapt after her, but in a heartbeat, she was gone, leaving only a shallow dip in the desert. Fine sand trickled into the hollow. Tom balled his fists in frustration. *I've lost her*. He broke into a run. *I have to warn the king!*

Tom ran on tired legs over the desert towards the distant coach. Eventually, panting and sweating, Tom closed on the king's party – half a dozen armed soldiers flanking a gilded carriage pulled by six sturdy carthorses. On seeing Tom, one soldier let out a cry of alarm and the horses lurched to a halt. The other guards swept forwards, brandishing their swords, forming a line between the king's carriage and Tom.

"Stay back!" one man cried.

"I need to speak with the king," Tom rasped, his voice coming out breathless and weak. He suddenly felt keenly aware of his sweat-drenched clothes and dusty skin. *I must look more like a mad man than a Master of the Beasts!* he thought. "It's me! Tom!" he said, panting. "The king's in danger!" The man who had spoken peered more closely through his helmet's visor.

"Tom?" he said. "I would hardly have known you!" At the same moment, the door to the carriage creaked open, and Hugo stepped blinking into the sun.

When he saw Tom, his brow creased into a worried frown. "Give him some water!" Hugo ordered his guards. Then he hurried to where Tom stood with his hands on his knees, gasping for breath.

"There's a Beast…on the loose," Tom panted. "It's…headed your way."

The king ran his eyes over the empty desert, still frowning anxiously. "Where?" he said. "What kind of Beast?" A guard thrust a canteen of water into Tom's hand. Tom drank deeply, then met the king's worried gaze.

"Malvel has summoned a giant spider Beast," Tom said. "It's under the desert, burrowing towards us. It could surface any moment."

The king paled. Then he clenched his jaw, his expression suddenly fierce. "If there is a Beast on the loose, we must stop it reaching this carriage," he growled. Hugo stepped to the coach and drew a silk curtain from the window. Queen Aroha sat inside, resting back against cushions, her expression serene. Tom's blood turned to ice. A swaddled baby was cradled in the queen's arms. *I thought they were safe in Tangala!* Aroha turned to the window.

"Tom?" the queen said, smiling faintly. "What are you doing here?"

"Your Highness," Tom stammered, fighting for composure. "A Beast is

near. But while there is blood in my
veins, I won't let it harm you."

The queen tensed. Her expression

hardened, and she sat up straight. One hand fell to the hilt of her sword, lying on the seat beside her, while the other still rested on the head of her baby. "While there's blood in *my* veins," she said in a low, angry voice, her green eyes flashing, "nothing shall harm my child!"

Tom nodded, lifting his own blade and turning to face the open desert.

"Surround the carriage!" the king ordered his men. "We're under attack!" The six armoured men swung into position, their armour blazing white in the sun.

Tom and Hugo stood side by side before the coach, gazing out over the scorched dunes. For a long, tense

time nothing stirred. Then Tom
spotted a dark blotch approaching
through the sky. He called on the
power of his golden helmet and felt a
rush of relief.

"It's Elenna on Storm," he told the
king, pointing. But his relief quickly
turned to alarm. He could feel a
subtle shifting beneath his feet – a
vibration deep down in the earth.

"The carriage is shaking!" Aroha
cried.

Tom spun to see the coach lurch,
the sand beneath it quaking. The
carthorses snorted and whinnied
with fear and Tom heard one of
Hugo's soldiers mutter a curse.

Tarantix is here!

THE ROYAL BABY IN PERIL

Tom threw up his arms to shield his face as a torrent of red sand erupted beneath him. Screams and crashes rang out in the chaos. When the sand cloud cleared, the Beast stood crouched before them, her vast white body gleaming in the sun and her black eyes glittering with spite. Behind her, the royal carriage lay on its side. *The queen and her baby!* The horses, having wrenched free of their harnesses, were already thundering away across the desert.

"Aroha!" Hugo cried, heedless of

the Beast, diving towards the fallen
coach. With a clack of jointed limbs,
the Beast shifted to crouch before
the king, ready to attack. Hugo's
soldiers charged into her path,
swords flashing. The Beast reared

back with a hiss.

"Keep her at bay!" Tom told the king's men, lunging after Hugo. Already, the king was tugging at the fallen carriage's door.

"It won't budge!" he cried. From inside the coach Tom could hear the baby wailing. And through the window, he could see the queen struggling to free herself from a tumble of cushions and bags, while clutching the infant.

"I'll get you out!" Tom told her. The clash of steel on bony hide rang out from behind them as Tom heaved at the door's bent handle. Nothing happened. He called on the strength of his breastplate and yanked. The

handle wrenched off in his hand.
Tom cast it aside. *CRUNCH!* One
of Tarantix's curved claws crashed
down right beside the carriage,
splintering the wooden shaft that
had harnessed the horses.

"Stay back!" a soldier roared,
driving a spear at the Beast's head.
It glanced off the Beast's hard
carapace.

"Take the baby!" Aroha cried, her
eyes glistening with fear. "There's no
time for me to get free!" She thrust
the screaming bundle through the
carriage window into Hugo's arms.
A soldier fell to the ground beside
the carriage with a cry of pain.

They can't keep the Beast at bay

much longer! Tom glanced over his shoulder to see Elenna soaring towards them on Storm. "I'll keep him safe," he said to Hugo. "Trust me!"

The king tensed, but as Tarantix let out a hideous scream of rage, he nodded. "Get him out of here, Tom. Quickly!"

Tom took the howling baby. "I'll come back for you."

He called on the power of his golden leg armour, ducked his head and ran from the battle, his heart clenching at the thought of leaving the king and queen at the Beast's mercy.

"Elenna, here!" he cried.

She lifted a hand as she spotted him, then swooped in to land. As soon as Storm's hooves touched down, Tom held out the bundle in his arms. "Take the baby to the palace," he said.

Elenna's eyes widened with shock. But she took the child gently and cradled him to her shoulder. She tapped her heels against Storm's sides, and the stallion leapt into the sky. "Be careful, Tom!" she called as Storm powered away.

Tom let out a breath of relief. *At least one royal is out of harm's way!* But when he looked back towards Tarantix, his guts twisted with horror and he threw himself into a desperate run. The Beast stood astride Aroha's carriage, trampling and tearing at the wood with her claws. *The queen will be crushed!* The king and his men jabbed up at the huge spider's belly and slashed at her limbs but already two soldiers lay squirming on the sand covered in sticky black silk.

As Tom drew close, he let out a battle cry, and leapt. He landed in a crouch on the spider's broad back and drove the tip of his sword downwards as hard as he could. The blade bit deep, and Tarantix reared with a screech. Tom's stomach flipped. He half jumped, half tumbled from the Beast's back and landed awkwardly beside the splintered remains of the coach.

From the corner of his eye Tom saw something move among the broken planks. He felt a rush of relief. *Thank goodness!* Through

what was left of the carriage
window Aroha's pale arm reached
upwards. *She's alive!* Tom threw
himself on to the wreckage of the
coach, tearing at the splintered
boards, wrenching them aside. He

glanced back to see a soldier lunge
for the Beast's rear leg and hack
at it, making the spider stagger.
Tarantix turned on the man with
a hiss as Aroha heaved herself
into the open. She looked pale and
shaken, but, apart from cuts and
grazes, unhurt.

"He's safe?" she asked.

Tom nodded. "Elenna's taking him
to the palace."

The queen staggered to her feet
and lifted her sword. "That thing is
going to pay!"

The Beast stood tall on her four
hind legs, towering over the king
and his last few soldiers with her
forelimbs spread wide, ready to

attack. Tom and Aroha charged together. The queen slashed at one of the Beast's rear legs, chopping it in half. Tom hacked at another. The rearing spider lurched and crouched down on its remaining limbs, screeching in fury.

Tom and Aroha darted past her to stand with the king and his men. Splotches of tarry gloop blackened the sand at their feet. Four of Hugo's soldiers were down now, covered in the stuff – only two remained.

Tarantix reared up once more, glaring down at Tom, her raised claws snapping hungrily. Her missing legs were beginning to grow back already. *Time to end this!* Tom raced forward, sword swinging.

Thwack! His sword sliced across the Beast's abdomen, leaving a deep score in the bone. Tarantix hissed and sent a jet of inky silk spurting towards him. Tom danced out of range while Aroha and the king charged side by side, slashing at the Beast's pale belly. A leg flicked out, knocking Aroha's blow aside. Another whipped down towards the king, snatching him up in a three-toed claw and tossing him roughly aside. King Hugo hit the ground with a grunt and lay still.

"No!" Aroha cried, racing to her husband's side and bending over him. Hugo's remaining soldiers both charged at once, letting out fierce roars. A spurt of stinking sludge slammed into them, lashing them together. They toppled to the ground, struggling against the slime.

Tarantix's curved fangs rasped together. She towered above Tom, forelimbs spread wide, and he heard her laughing voice in his mind. *You cannot beat me! I will feast on your flesh!*

"You can feast on this!" Tom cried. Using the power of his golden boots, he leapt up towards her head, his sword flashing in a glittering arc, straight for her hideous eyes.

SMACK! A bony limb slammed into Tom's chest, swatting him aside.

His neck whiplashed and his vision
blurred as he tumbled through
the air. He landed hard and rolled
himself into a ball, clutching his ribs
and gasping for air.

Through his swirling vision, Tom saw Aroha rise from the king's side. The queen let out a bloodcurdling scream and swept forward. Her sword flashed out at the same time as one of the Beast's white limbs swiped downwards. Sword and bone met with a sickening crack. Tarantix's limb splintered, but the force of the blow sent the queen's blade spinning from her hand.

Aroha leapt towards her sword, but suddenly yelped and lurched to one side, her feet trapped in a pool of black sludge. The Beast's claw whipped out and caught her across the temple. Her eyelids fluttered and she crumpled to the ground. A surge of anger pushed Tom to his feet despite his dizziness and pain

Mine! the Beast hissed, driving her curved fangs downwards towards the queen. Tom bent his shoulder and cannoned desperately into the Beast's lowered head. Tarantix's fangs jabbed down into the sand just a fraction from Aroha's chest.

With a tremendous screech Tarantix lifted her head and reared up to her full height. Tom stumbled back out of reach of her clawed feet, but as he moved, the spider jabbed the pointed tip of her abdomen towards him, releasing a spurt of black silk. The goo slammed into Tom's chest and wrapped around him, lashing his arms to his sides and squeezing tight.

The Beast's front limbs clacked and whirred together in a blur of motion, reeling Tom in. Without his hands to break his fall, Tom toppled face first into the sand. Grit filled his nose and mouth as the Beast tugged him towards her. Tom squirmed, managing to heave himself on to his back. Spitting and shaking his head to clear the sand, he looked up to see the Beast towering over him, her white fangs glinting in the sun. Reflected back at him over and over in her cluster of gleaming eyes, he could see his own terrified face. With a sudden jerk, Tom was yanked up from the ground towards Tarantix's waiting fangs.

I'm not dying like this! Tom strained against the bonds around his chest, but with his arms wrapped so tightly, all he could do was buck and writhe, dangling in the air. Tarantix's fangs parted, revealing her pale, waxy mouthparts chomping hungrily together.

Tom bent double, kicking his legs upwards. He planted his feet either side of the spider's glistening maw. He could hear a slurping, sucking noise coming from inside. The bristly hairs that covered the Beast's pale flesh quivered excitedly. Tom pushed with all his strength, but already his

muscles burned.

I'm not going to make it! Tom
realised. He thought of the king
and queen both lying injured below
him. Of what Malvel would do the
kingdom once Tom was dead. *At*

least the royal baby is safe... Tom told himself, but in his heart, he knew it wasn't enough. He'd failed Avantia and he'd failed himself. He could feel his legs buckling.

And now he was going to die.

DUEL IN THE DESERT

Tom swallowed hard, his heart thudding against his bound ribs and his legs shaking with the effort of forcing the Beast's chomping mouth away.

I have never tasted a Master of the Beasts before! Tarantix's voice rasped in his mind. Her pale

mouthparts munched together
with a hideous slurp. Tom suddenly
spotted a huge blot in the sky
beyond her, moving unsteadily on
flailing wings. *A bird? No! Far too
big.* Tom felt a rush of hope as he
made out a lashing tail and blazing
eyes. *Ferno!* The dragon lurched
from side to side as he flew, as
if still waking from his slumber,
but he was getting closer by the
moment, banking sharply. With his
renewed hope, Tom found a sudden
burst of strength.

"You won't taste me!" Tom told
the Beast. "You'll never eat again!"
Ferno's vast shadow fell across
them. The dragon opened his jaws

and sent a burst of orange flames towards Tarantix's rear legs.

Tom gasped at the searing blast of

heat. He felt the Beast's grip on him loosen as flames crackled up around her. His stomach lurched as he fell, then hit the ground and rolled away, yanking his arms free of the sticky strands still clinging to his chest.

Tarantix shrieked and writhed, beating her blazing limbs against the ground. Flames licked at her body. Tom scrabbled to his feet and snatched up his sword from where he had dropped it when he fell. Wreathed in fire, the Beast threw herself down on the sand and rolled over and over. Smoke billowed up from her body in waves until the sand quenched the flames. Ferno swooped low overhead, wobbling as he flew. Tom felt the ground shake as the dragon landed, lurched to one side then collapsed in a heap of leathery wings. *He's still weak from the poison!* Tom realised. Gratitude swelled in his chest. *But he came anyway.*

As Tarantix rose on blackened limbs and turned towards him, Tom saw dark scorch marks covering her underbelly and sides. Where the bone had charred, it looked brittle and dry, laced with tiny cracks. But her glittering eyes and curved fangs hadn't been touched by the flames. Her claws clacked together viciously and she glared down at Tom, black eyes bulging with hate.

A three-toed claw lashed out. Tom
was ready for it, poised on the balls
of his feet. He ducked his head and
raced beneath her. With two hands
on his sword hilt, he drove the blade
upwards into the fire-singed bone of
her belly. It sank deep into Tarantix's

charred, brittle hide. Through the
hilt, Tom felt her shudder.

Tom twisted the blade and tugged
it free, leaping back as a torrent
of stinking black filth poured
out from a widening crack in the
Beast's abdomen. The stench of it

made Tom stagger, bile rising in his throat. Tarantix hissed, drawing her limbs beneath her, crumpling into a ball. Still more vile gloop poured from her body, making a tarry pool all around her. The pool started to swirl. Tom staggered away from the edge of it, watching in horrified shock as the Beast let out a thin, high shriek. Then, like a plug pulled from a tub, the gloop funnelled away into the ground, sucking the spider down with it until nothing remained but empty sand. Tom stared at the bare patch of desert, anger and pity growing inside him. *Malvel brought the Beast here to kill me or to suffer this. I'll make sure he pays.*

A now familiar, black stone column burst upwards from the centre of the dip in the sand,

climbing higher until it towered far above Tom. The magical totem cast a slender beam of shadow eastwards across the desert.

The sight filled Tom with weary dread. *The next stage of our Quest...*

Tom heard a groan, then the clank of armour. He turned to see Hugo's fallen men beginning to stir. The black webbing binding their arms had vanished with the Beast. Hugo and Aroha stood clutching one another.

"We must get to the palace," the queen said.

Tom glanced around at the injured soldiers and shattered coach. Beyond them Ferno was already flying unsteadily towards the horizon, gaining height as his leathery wings beat the air. Tom touched the red jewel at his belt. "Thank you, friend, you saved my life," he told the Beast, "but we need more help. Can you carry us to the palace?"

Ferno didn't reply – and Tom couldn't feel the Beast's presence in his mind. *Not surprising, really – Malvel's potion is still leaving him.* As Tom watched the wavering path of the Beast's flight, he felt a stab of despair. *He's too sick to carry us all, anyway…*

But in the distance, Tom could see the silhouettes of the carthorses, returning now the Beast had gone. *Six horses, nine people*, Tom counted. And several of the soldiers were limping or holding bleeding cuts as they gazed in wonder at the magical totem.

Tom glanced at the shadow path, and then again at the sorry, ragtag state of the group. A cold finger of dread traced his spine. He knew that every moment he delayed in his Quest, Malvel would unleash more evil on Avantia. But Tom also knew he couldn't leave the king's party to fend for themselves.

I need to get everyone to the palace somehow. Tom thought of Elenna and Storm, flying ahead of them with the baby. *At least I know the royal heir is safe in their hands.* Tom forced his shoulders back and took a deep breath, then met the queen's worried gaze.

"Elenna will take good care of

your baby," Tom said. "It's going to be tough, but working together, we'll all get home as well."

Hugo looked pale. "With Malvel on the loose, the fate of Avantia depends on our speed," said the king.

Tom nodded. The Quest had become a race against time.

THE END

CONGRATULATIONS, YOU HAVE COMPLETED THIS QUEST!

At the end of each chapter you were
awarded a special gold coin.
The QUEST in this book was
worth an amazing 8 coins.

Look at the Beast Quest totem picture
inside the back cover of this book to
see how far you've come in your journey
to become

MASTER OF THE BEASTS.

The more books you read,
the more coins you will collect!

Do you want your own
Beast Quest Totem?

1. Cut out and collect the coin below
2. Go to the Beast Quest website
3. Download and print out your totem
4. Add your coin to the totem
www.beastquest.co.uk/totem

Don't miss the next exciting Beast Quest book, LYPIDA THE SHADOW FIEND!

Read on for a sneak peek...

TERRIBLE NEWS

"There it is!" cried Tom, reining in his horse as it crested the hilltop. In the distance, the City glimmered against the evening sky, lit by a hundred torches that flickered from the battlements.

A murmur of relief ran around the royal retinue. The soldiers were slumped wearily over their saddles and many nursed wounds. It had been over a day's hard ride from the Ruby Desert, where Tarantix the Bone Spider had attacked the royal party on its way back from Tangala.

"At last!" gasped King Hugo, embracing Queen Aroha tightly. They were both mounted on a single horse, their royal clothes tattered and streaked with dust.

"We're not there yet," the queen replied. She slapped the horse's rump and it bolted down the hillside towards the City, hooves thundering.

Tom grinned. The queen's baby was

waiting for them back in the palace, carried to safety by Elenna when Tarantix had attacked.

"Let's go!" Tom cried, his body filled with a fresh energy.

The sky was almost black as they reached the palace walls. Standing just above the gate was the familiar figure of Captain Harkman, torchlight glinting off his helmet. "Lower the drawbridge!" the captain shouted.

At once it swung down. King Hugo and Queen Aroha went first, followed closely by Tom and the soldiers. Tom felt a warm rush of relief to be back at the palace.

In the centre of the courtyard stood

Elenna, awkwardly holding a baby
bundled to her chest. Queen Aroha
swung herself from the saddle and
rushed to take the child.

"Thank you!" she said, tears coming to her eyes.

King Hugo clapped Elenna on the back. "How can we ever thank you? You saved our son!"

Elenna caught Tom's eye, and winked. "It wasn't just me," she said. "We all did our bit. I'm just glad he's safe – and you are too!"

"That reminds me," said Hugo, turning to look at the injured soldiers clambering down from their horses. "Get these men to the healers at once!"

As Captain Harkman's soldiers took away the wounded, Tom dismounted and watched the king and queen's happy reunion with their son. He knew he had done the right thing by escorting them back to the palace, but even so he felt uneasy. *They're safe now, but for how long?* Malvel had a head start, and he would surely be using the *Book of Derthsin* to summon another Beast from the Netherworld. *I need to return to my Quest!*

"Are you thinking what I'm thinking?" asked Elenna, as she came to Tom's side. "We need to get after the Dark Wizard, and quickly!"

Tom nodded. "Where's Storm?"

"He's being fed and watered," Elenna said. "I'll show you."

As the two of them set off towards the stable, Daltec stepped out of an archway. The gangly young wizard raised a robed arm in greeting.

"Tom!" he said. "What a relief to see you safe and sound!"

A girl appeared behind him, dressed in red, with short dark hair and delicate butterfly wings fluttering at her back. It was Lyra, the Henkrallian witch. She was helping a hunched figure shuffle towards them, as he leaned heavily on a walking stick.

Tom gasped. "I can't believe it!"

Aduro's wrinkled face was almost as white as his beard, but the twinkle was back in his eyes.

"You're better!" Tom cried. Malvel had cast a spell on the former

wizard, sending him into a magical
sleep.

　"I'm not quite my old self yet,"

Aduro admitted. "But I couldn't miss the chance to greet you two heroes!"

Tom and Elenna wrapped the old man up in a hug.

"I don't know what we'd do without you," said Elenna, as they broke apart.

"It's all thanks to Daltec and Lyra," said Aduro. "They saved my life."

"I'm not sure I'd go that far," said Daltec, blushing. But he was grinning proudly all the same.

Read
LYPIDA THE SHADOW FIEND
to find out what happens next!

Fight the Beasts,
Fear the Magic

Do you want to know more
about BEAST QUEST?
Then join our Quest Club!

Visit
www.beastquest.co.uk/club
and sign up today!

Are you a collector of the Beast Quest Cards?
Visit the website for further information.

Beast Quest

AVAILABLE SPRING 2018

The epic adventure is brought to life on **Xbox One** and **PS4** for the first time ever!

www.maximumgames.com   www.beast-quest.com